THE SECRET

What was Kerim's secret? Jeff wondered. The Arab boy stood guard over the dark and dangerous cave, shielding it as though his life depended on it.

Jeff wanted to be Kerim's friend, but something always seemed to scare the other boy away. Had Jeff seen too much? Was he now in danger, too?

Jeff's family had come to explore the mysteries in the sandy slopes of Israel's Tel Gezer, the archaeological site of a burial mound dating back to Bible times. But all too soon Jeff uncovered a mystery of his own. Before he had time to catch his breath and decide what to do, his secret became a nightmare which plunged him into an adventure he would never forget!

THE OTHER SIDE OF THE TELL

Bettie Wilson Story

Illustrated by Seymour Fleishman

David C. Cook Publishing Co.

ELGIN, ILLINOIS—WESTON, ONTARIO
LA HABRA, CALIFORNIA

David C. Cook Publishing Co., Elgin, IL 60120

Printed in the United States of America
Library of Congress Catalog Number: 76-1548
ISBN: 0-912692-92-8

ACKNOWLEDGMENTS

I am deeply indebted to my husband, Geoffrey L. Story, Jr., Chairman of the Department of Religion, Illinois Wesleyan University, whose experience in Israel made this book possible. The location for this story is Tel Gezer where he participated in an archaeological excavation. The historical background, geographical location, and archaeological findings included in this story are true to the Tel Gezer site, although fictional descriptions of the Tell itself do occur.

My thanks are due Madeleine L'Engle and Penny Anderson for their helpful criticism and suggestions for revision.

I am also indebted to the Indiana University Foundation for fellowship assistance in the completion of this work.

TABLE OF CONTENTS

The Tell

1

The Tell

IT WAS LATE AFTERNOON in early July. The desert sun zeroed in on us so strong that I sometimes felt we were trapped in an oven. Finally our rented car turned off a highway in Israel. The trip through the mountains from Jerusalem was behind us and we bumped up and down on a dirt road in the foothills. I pointed to a deep blue band beyond the plains below us.

"Is that the Mediterranean Sea or just the sky?"

Mom and Dad answered at the same time. "It's the Mediterranean."

"I see the tell! I see the tell!" Jennifer screamed.

Dad pressed his ear and apologized to the driver.

"It's just another hill—not the tell," Mom explained.

"Jennifer, if you don't stop bouncing on this seat, I'm going to . . ."

"Now, Jeff," Dad said, "we celebrated your 12th birthday yesterday, so grow up a little."

My parched tongue stuck to my teeth like skin to dry ice. I rubbed the dust on my arm up into little dirt balls. Why didn't Dad stop Jennifer when she yelled at me? Besides, I *was* growing up, and I was excited, too. Sometimes my chest tightened up so much I could hardly breathe, but I wasn't ruining the springs in the car seat or bursting eardrums.

When we passed through a tiny farm village, the driver pushed back his cap and pointed ahead. Just on the edge of the plains lay the tell.

"It looks like a long hill with a flat top." Jennifer sounded disappointed.

"But it's not a natural hill," Dad said in his teacher voice. "It's a mound made of the ruins of many cities over several centuries. It's like a layer cake that must be lifted off layer by layer."

"Why?"

"To discover, Jen, all we can about the ancient peoples who lived here. Each layer represents a period of years—perhaps even centuries."

Our dad and mom taught at a university in Illinois during the school year, but here they were going to be plain old volunteers for a month on an archaeological dig.

The road wound along the length of the tell. I

gazed up its slope, licking my cracked lips. This time I nearly jumped on the seat myself.

"There's a cave!" I shouted.

"Where? Where?"

"In the side of the hill!"

The driver eased the car over the bumps and rocks in the road.

"Can I get out, Dad? Please?"

"Jeff, you can't go in the cave alone so you may as well stay in the car."

Mom's lips and forehead puckered up into a frown. "Mr. McDowell wasn't sure such young kids ought to come, and here you want to run off alone before we—"

"Don't you trust me, Mom?"

The car stopped.

Before Mom could answer—I knew what she would say anyway—I opened the door and ran to move two huge stones that blocked the road. My chest tightened. I wanted to dash up just to look at that cave so bad I could taste it.

I straightened up and called, "I'll meet you at the top!"

I sprinted out across the rocky ground toward the cave before Dad could call me back. I turned once and waved as the car followed the road slowly toward the other end of the tell. Good old driver! He kept right on going. My parents did not look happy, but Jennifer was sitting there waving her hand off.

13

When I crawled up to the cave which was several yards from the top, a boy—he scared me silly just standing there—faced me just inside the dark entrance. I couldn't understand a word he said, but he motioned for me to move away. That was funny.

"Why can't I go inside?" I wasn't really planning on it after what Dad had said, but when this strange boy blocked the entrance, I was tempted.

"You can go in with me," I begged. With him I wouldn't be alone.

He didn't understand. I pointed stupidly and tried to see inside the cave. No sunlight invaded it. I saw nothing.

The boy said nothing. He was about my height, but thinner. His black eyes stayed glued to my face.

"What is your name?"

His eyes flickered once. "Kerim," he said.

So! He understood.

"I want to know why I can't go inside."

Again he said nothing. We stared at each other.

"Jeff! There you are!" Jennifer slid partway down the hill.

"Jennifer, will you leave me alone?"

"Dad wants you. The tents are way at the other end, and he needs you to help get our stuff unpacked."

"I told him I'd meet you at the top."

"But he thought—"

"I know, I know. He thought I went in the cave alone, didn't he?"

"He didn't say so."

"He doesn't need to."

Jennifer edged back up the distance she had come down from the top, taking two steps and sliding back one. "And, anyway, I was curious about the cave, too."

That strange Kerim still stared at me. I wasn't the kind to fight to get inside, but I sure did want to know why he was guarding it.

He stood in the shade of the cave entrance while the sun beat down on me. I was dying of thirst. Finally I gave up and scuffed up the hill to join Jennifer.

"You stick your nose in everything I do," I grumbled. "If you hadn't come along, I bet I could have had at least a look inside."

I gazed out over the flat surface of the mound. This end, probably two or more city blocks long, was covered with trenches where the archaeological team was digging. At the other end were the living tents, a water tower, and a bunch of sheds covered with tin roofs. There was not one single shade tree on this whole desert tell.

Ibriks and Sherds

2

Ibriks and Sherds

A STRANGE THING HAPPENED the next morning. Somebody in the family woke up before me. It was Jennifer.

I did not even hear the artillery-shell gong sound at four a.m. Jennifer shook me awake. "Get up, lazy!"

I lunged out in the dark to push her away.

"Miss me—miss me! Now you got to kiss me!"

"Oh, Jen, stop that baby stuff," I answered, pushing back up on my bunk.

"All right, Jeff," Dad said. "It's only four o'clock in the morning. You have 20 minutes till breakfast."

Ugh! How could I eat at that time of day? Work started early and ended at noon because the sun's heat was supposed to be unbearable most of the afternoon. I lay still, hugging to myself the last warm quiet second in my sleeping bag, then wiggled out of it and into my clothes. Jennifer was already dressed.

There were four long rows of sleeping tents; ours was at the end nearest the dining shed. We didn't have far to walk for our breakfast—three peanut butter sandwiches.

"I'll get up early every morning for these," I said to no one in particular, and discovered that most of the 125 others were too sleepy to talk.

"Where are most of them from?" I asked Mom.

"Most of them are Americans, Jeff, both Christian and Jewish volunteers from universities and churches all over the country. There are also a lot of Jewish people from right here in Israel, and Arab Bedouin who live here too."

I looked up and down the long table. "I met a boy, Kerim, at the cave yesterday. I don't see him now."

Hank, a college student from Colorado who looked as if he considered it worth a trophy that he had gotten out of bed so early, gazed at me with his baggy eyes.

He said, "Kerim lives out on the plain. He's one of the Bedouin tribe. He can disappear and reappear the quickest of anybody I know, but he'll be around here somewhere. You kids ought to get together and find something to do."

Kids! Everywhere I turned on this tell somebody was reminding me of how young I was, as if I was a puny third-grader like Jennifer. I concentrated on eating my sandwiches.

By five o'clock everyone had passed through the gates to the unfenced area of the tell where they all went to work in the trenches that had been assigned to them the afternoon before.

Mom suggested that Jennifer go back to our tent and sleep.

"No! I'm too excited," she said. "I don't want to go to bed."

Mom glanced at me. I didn't want to look after Jennifer, so I said, "I gotta find Dad," and headed toward the cave where he was going to work.

When I saw Kerim standing at the entrance, I stopped, remembering that Dad said I could not go in alone. Since Kerim didn't seem to speak English, I couldn't talk him into going inside with me. All the cave workers must have already entered. I glanced up at the rim of the mound and saw Hank.

"You better get your *ibrik!*" he yelled. "You'll need it pretty soon."

"Are you coming down here?" Maybe he would go in the cave with me.

"Nope, I work on the top."

Just my luck! There was nobody I could follow into the cave. Kerim ignored me.

"Your *ibrik!*" Hank shouted again before leaving the edge of the tell.

The leaders said last night that we had to drink

lots of water to keep from being dehydrated, so I took the long trek back to the gates, inside the fenced-in living area, and to a shed for a jug.

I filled the clay jug. *Ibrik* was a nicer word than jug; it was also the first Arabic word I had learned. It worked like a desert bag, keeping the water inside as cool as if it had just come from a spring. Carrying it, I headed back again.

"What're you doing scratching through that mound of pottery?" I demanded of Jennifer as I passed her.

"That man said I could."

"Don't point!"

She went back to scratching.

I glanced at the man—Mr. McDowell, one of the professional archaeologists. His stern eyes, dark brown like cocoa, and his thick black beard reminded me again that Jennifer and I were the youngest ones there. Mr. Mac had probably let us come against his "better judgment" as Mom would say. Finally he spoke in a gravelly voice that made me pay attention.

"That's just the discard pile. She may have any of those sherds she wants."

"Sherds?"

"That's what we call pottery pieces. It really comes from the word 'potsherd' or 'the broken pieces of a pot.' "

"Oh!" Jennifer held up a triangular piece. "This one has designs. Don't you want to keep it?"

"What're you doing scratching through that pottery?" Jeff demanded.

Nosy Jen. If he wanted to keep it, would it be on the discard pile? It really was pretty. I wished I had found it myself.

Mr. McDowell said, "We have other pieces of that type which are even more distinctive."

"I can really keep it?"

"Of course, since it came from the discards. No one may keep anything that's found on the tell until we have had a chance to decide if we need it or not. If we don't need it, it goes on this discard pile, so take anything you like."

Jennifer rubbed the designed piece with her fingers. "I feel sorry for discards; nobody wants them," she said and started scratching in the pile again as if determined to save more of the broken pieces.

"Young fellow, you should get a cap or handkerchief on your head. That sun isn't merciful," Mr. Mac said.

For Pete's sake, it wasn't even seven o'clock yet. Miss Perfect patted the cap on her head and grinned at me. She was asking for it today.

"I'll get one," I muttered and headed for our tent.

"You look like Abraham Lincoln," I heard Jennifer say to Mr. McDowell. Brother! What would he say to that? To my surprise, he laughed.

"Does everyone with a black beard remind you of Lincoln?"

"Oh, no, Sir. Only you."

I walked out of hearing range so missed his answer, but Jennifer was laughing with him. I wished I did not keep remembering the sternness of his eyes.

Inside our tent I stuck my thumb into the handle of my *ibrik*, rested the base on my shoulder as I had seen others do, and drank from it. I rubbed the moisture collected on the outside onto my face. It felt cool and good.

After I found my cap I wandered around from area to area watching the volunteers. They were not finding anything much as far as I could tell. Walking to the rim of the mound, I noticed that Kerim was still guarding the cave entrance. I sat on the ground and threw pebbles down the slope and stared at the Bedouin camp on the plain at the base of our tell. I counted 18 black tents which Dad said were made of goatskin or woven from rough wool. Kerim lived there, so Hank had said, and I wondered if he lived inside or outside the area fenced in by cactus plants. Camels lounged inside the cactus enclosure, but some older children had taken the goats and sheep out to pasture in the foothills of the mountains.

I saw the women spinning and weaving and caring for the smaller children. From that camp the men left every morning for work—a few on the tell, others down in the rich farm valley. I wondered if the life of these Bedouin was different from the nomads I read about in the Bible. They looked as if they had lived this way thousands of years. If Kerim knew a little English, I could ask him.

By 8:30 a.m. when work stopped for our second breakfast of eggs, cheese, yogurt, tomatoes, and fruit, it was already getting hot. And I was beginning to wonder how long a month would be with 123 adults, Miss Perfect, and an Arab boy I could not understand.

Who Needs a Sister Around?

3

Who Needs a Sister Around?

I WANTED TO HELP with the digging. Sure, I knew volunteers must be at least 18 years old, but since I was here I figured I could do the real work too. Mom, with a small hand trowel, was working with others in a limited square area, carefully measuring and recording each level as they dug. It looked simple enough.

"Why won't Mr. Mac let me be a dirt archaeologist and help dig, Mom? Maybe I could find something exciting—a whole pottery bowl, coins, or an old tool—or something."

Mom wiped her face on a blouse sleeve. "You're really too young, Jeff, but whether or not you can help may depend on how responsible you can prove to be."

I picked up a rock and flung it angrily off the

side of the tell. I did not want to have to prove myself to anybody. I was having a hard enough time trying to get my parents to trust me.

"Why don't you suggest to them that I can help?"

"I can't tell them. You must show them by being careful with chores, attending the evening lectures, and—"

"Then, I might as well give up."

"I didn't mean to discourage you, Jeff. There are lots of things you can do. How about getting a goofer bucket to collect discards for us? We have a lot of dirt and stones to move out of here."

On my way back to the sheds at the other end of the tell, I walked the rim and checked the cave entrance again. Kerim was not there! I ran down the hill. At the entrance I stopped and listened. No sounds reached me. I stepped inside to see if I could find Dad and the other workers. As I moved cautiously ahead, the cave curved suddenly and plunged me into darkness.

I stopped and listened again but could hear only my heart thudding against my chest. I drank from my *ibrik* and wiped the sweat off my face with my shirttail. Sliding my feet on the ground, I inched along perhaps three more steps. I could not see my hand two inches in front of my face. I thought about Carol, the blind girl in my school back home, and wondered if her blindness was as black as this cave. I turned around and trudged back to the entrance. The bright sunlight blinded me in a different way.

"Scaredy-cat!"

Jennifer stared down at me from the top of the tell.

"Quit following me around! Go back to the tents."

"I don't want to!"

If I made her go she would run crying to Mom and, as usual, Mom would think I should look out for her. Being a big brother sure is a pain—in more ways than one. I couldn't let her see that the dark cave really had scared me.

"Listen, Jenni-*fur*, have you been drinking water like you're supposed to?"

She straightened proudly. "Nope!"

"Didn't you hear what Mr. McDowell said last night?" I asked as I climbed the hill to her.

"What?"

"About how the sizzling sun dehydrates us and we have to keep an *ibrik* of water with us all the time and drink, drink, drink. Why aren't you doing it?"

"I dunno."

I handed her my *ibrik*. "Drink!"

She did, her big brown eyes wide and questioning. I better scare her plenty so she would remember what to do.

"If you let the sun shrink all the water out of you, you'll turn into a goofer!"

That made me remember Mom's request for a goofer bucket so I lit out for the gate and the supply sheds. Jennifer ran along right behind me.

"What do you mean, 'goofer'?"

"Just what I said."

"I don't want to be a goofer!" she wailed.

"You see this bucket? It's to pick up goofers!"

"How do you know?"

"I just know," I said, feeling important. "You ask Mom. She'll tell you this is a goofer bucket."

Jennifer grabbed my *ibrik* and drank to the bottom. "There!"

"Yeah, well, fill it up and bring it to me at Mom's square."

I ran down the length of the tell to deliver the bucket. I was relieved that Mom didn't say anything about the delay; she just pointed to the pile of debris that needed to be dumped in the nearby wheelbarrow. I started to work. Without my water supply it seemed that the sun was concentrating on me. Sweat dripped off my nose.

When I had filled the wheelbarrow, I pushed it to the dump pile. Since there was no shade tree, I plopped down on a big rock and gazed out over the plain toward Tel Aviv 15 miles away. I sniffed the air for a Mediterranean Sea breeze and snuffed up dusty heat instead. Off in the opposite direction were the mountains we had driven through yesterday.

I was beginning to like this land. It felt different, I guess, because people had lived here for so many thousands of years.

Dad told me that the month before we arrived, the archaeological team had discovered some 15th century B.C. burial mounds in the cave. That seemed like a long time ago, but groups of peoples had lived here as long as 2,800 years before the birth of Christ. That meant people had been right here where I was sitting almost 4,000 years ago. Fire or disease or hostile tribes might cause the people to leave; then maybe for 100 years or more no one would live here. Later the city would be rebuilt. I could hardly believe King Solomon had lived here about 950 years before Jesus lived in this land.

I wondered if the sun was this hot back in those days. Maybe that's why King David sang, "He leads me beside still waters." I supposed the *sun* hadn't changed much. It gave me a sort of funny feeling that I was living where once King Solomon had lived and in the land of David. It made them *real*!

Jennifer appeared, drank from my *ibrik* she was carrying, and handed it to me.

"Why don't you carry your own *ibrik*?" I asked as she sat on the ground beside me.

"You can share, Jeff. You want a goofer for a sister?"

I gulped down the water. "Sometimes I don't want a sister around," I said crossly.

33

Her brown eyes widened. So what? Sometimes I felt just like that. Why couldn't I say it?

"Here!"

She dropped into my hand a curved piece of pottery which fit exactly into my palm. It was a glazed piece painted red. The designs looked like stick figures with a round ball and spokes standing out from it. Could that be a sun? It was the prettiest piece I had seen yet and she was giving it to me.

"Is this another one you dug out of the discard pile?"

She nodded and reached over to rub it with her thumb. Her soft brown hair brushed my cheek and her arm felt cool against mine. I held the pottery carefully and mumbled, "Thanks, Jen."

She stuck her chin in the air. "I'm giving it to you, Jeff, even though you don't like me. And I don't like you a bit either for what you said."

She stamped off, her small body stiff and proud. I rubbed the pottery with my finger. It was a fantastic piece and I didn't deserve it. I tucked it carefully in my shirt pocket; tonight I would keep it under my pillow.

Kerim

4

Kerim

I DID NOT WANT JENNIFER TO LEAVE after giving me this sherd so I called to her.

She stopped but didn't turn around.

"Come on back and sit beside me."

"OK." She hesitated, then bounced back as if she had forgotten all about our fuss. I hoped so.

A jet plane passed overhead, and she pointed to it. "*That* doesn't belong here!"

"It sure does," I said, eager to show off some of my knowledge. I tried to mock Dad's teacher voice. "Israel is just as modern as it is ancient. I bet Tel Aviv is as modern as Chicago."

"But look at the moabs down there!"

"Not moabs, Jen. Nomads! Bedouin. Can you say Bed-oh-in?"

"Yep. Bed-oh-in. What are Bed-oh-in?"

"They are people who move their families and

animals wherever they can find work and water. They don't live in one place all the time."

"Like the migrants that come to Illinois every summer?"

"Not exactly. Maybe like shepherds in the old days that were led to still waters." I was thinking about King David's song.

We sat and looked around us for a while. I finally said, "It's quiet here. Makes it hard to believe fighting is going on in other parts of Israel."

"Fighting? Is that why we saw soldiers in Jerusalem?"

"I guess so."

"Why are they fighting, Jeff?"

"I don't know exactly. Something about the Arabs living here for hundreds of years in this country they called Palestine. Then the United Nations gave Palestine to the Jewish people about 30 years ago and they call it Israel."

"My New Testament says the Jews lived here when Jesus did. He was a Jew."

"Sure, they lived here hundreds of years, too."

"Then what's the fuss?"

"Well, a lot of Arab guerrillas are trying to get their land back. And I guess the land really belongs to both sides."

"Gorillas? Real live gorillas? Like in a zoo?"

"For Pete's sake, Jen, these guerrillas are people. They fight other people."

"Are all Arabs gorillas?"

"Of course not, silly. Lots of Arabs live in Israel who aren't guerrillas. Kerim is an Arab."

"I don't understand. Nobody fights here. Everybody likes everybody."

"Yeah, we're all working together—the Bedouin Arabs, Jewish Israelis, and us Christians—and Jews—from other countries."

Jennifer pulled her cap down over her eyes. "Aren't the Arabs Christian?"

"Silly, they're Muslims." I was glad to get off the guerrilla subject because I had told her everything I knew.

"I'm not silly! We visited an Arab Lutheran hospital in Jerusalem. And Lutherans are Christians!"

I remembered that visit, but it was hard for me to give up my old idea that all Arabs were Muslims. I wondered if Kerim were a Muslim or a Christian. I surely was interested in him—partly because I wanted to figure out a way to talk with him—but mostly because he had kept me from entering the cave. I still wanted to know why.

"Jeff! Jennifer! Come here!" Mr. Nebergall, one of the field supervisors, was waving to us. We raced each other to the cooking shed.

"How about ringing everyone to dinner?"

"Oh, boy!" Jennifer grabbed a shovel leaning against the wall and swung at the long artillery shell which hung from the corner of the roof. She missed.

39

"I never saw a dinner gong like that!" she pouted.

"It's left over from the 1967 war," Mr. Nebergall said in a solemn tone. "Somehow I like its present use better—calling all of us from many countries to meals three times a day."

Jennifer did not miss the second time. The artillery shell bonged loud and clear all across the tell and probably over the plain and in and out of the mountains. The way she held that shovel you'd think she had just slain a giant.

I held my ears. "I'm deaf!"

"I want to do it again!"

Mr. Nebergall took the shovel. "There'll be other times. Thanks for helping."

"OK."

"Race you to the sinks!" Jennifer challenged me.

Kid games. She dashed off but I walked slowly toward the long row of metal lavatories to wash my hands. The tin roof over them gave little relief from the noon heat. Suddenly I realized it was smart to work in the early morning coolness and quit at noon before we fainted.

I wondered if I threw a handful of water into the air if it would evaporate before it could hit the ground. I wouldn't dare try it; our water supply was too precious. In fact, we were required to have a two weeks' supply of clothes so that instead of washing them here at the end of a week, our dirty clothes could be sent into Jerusalem to be washed. The water in our supply tanks was only for drinking and for washing ourselves and the pottery we unearthed. Nothing else— especially crazy experiments with heat.

I glanced into the tiny mirror when I finished washing and saw Kerim coming up from behind.

"Hi!" I said as he washed his hands next to me.

"Hello!"

I nearly fell off the tell. "Can you speak English?"

"I understand a little English," he said as if feeling out every word. His hair, in black wet waves, was plastered to his head. His dark eyes met mine in the mirror.

My words tumbled out. "Why didn't you talk to me at the cave? Why did you keep me out? Why—"

"I do not understand."

I drew a picture of the cave entrance in the air and repeated the same motions he had used when he signaled me to leave.

"Cave—" I said.

"Cave? The cave, you say, is there." He pointed toward the other side of the tell.

"I know—I know. But I want you to tell me—"

He shook his head violently. "I do not understand."

I decided he understood a lot more than he let on. During rest time after lunch, I meant to pump

41

Kerim stuffed some bread and fruit inside his shirt when he thought nobody was looking.

all the information I could about the cave from Dad.

I hardly knew what I ate. After lunch I saw Kerim stuff some bread and fruit in his shirt when he thought nobody was looking.

When Dad herded us off to our tent after lunch, Kerim ran down the side of the tell in the direction of the cave. I wanted to run after him. Instead I stumbled into a wheelbarrow and fell sprawling.

Jennifer giggled. "Better watch where you're going!"

"Why didn't you warn me?"

"I don't like you. Remember?"

Nobody, not even Jen, forgot my faults.

She picked up the pottery sherd she had given me which had fallen out of my shirt pocket and handed it to me. I rubbed my thumb over it as she had done earlier.

"Race you to the tent!" she said.

I decided to let her beat me. After all, I would never get to be a dirt archaeologist if I ended up with a sunstroke my first day out.

The Cave

5

The Cave

THE TENTS WERE ENORMOUS. I dreaded having to stay in ours for four hours. It was probably oven hot. I grabbed a towel and went for a cool shower. The shower stalls did not have any roofs—I wanted to glare at the sun. It was ruining my afternoon.

When I returned, a cool breeze off the Mediterranean Sea was sifting through the netting on the rolled-up sides of the tent.

"I bet the oak tree in our backyard would do wonders for this tell," I said as I plopped on my cot and gazed at the sky through the net patterns. The breeze felt as refreshing as the misty spray from Yosemite Falls when we had visited there once. I couldn't believe it could be so nice.

I scored zero with Dad when I asked him about the cave. They were working by lamplight deep inside, he said, to uncover more burial places *if* they existed. He had noticed nothing strange about the cave.

"That Arab boy acts like he's guarding it."

"You have an active imagination, Jeff, and I must remind you again that you may not venture alone inside the cave. If you want to, you may go with me tomorrow and see the excavations."

"OK." I'd settle for getting inside any way I could.

"What does Kerim do in the cave?" I asked.

There was no answer. Dad was breathing heavily, already disgustingly sound asleep. So was Jennifer.

Mom was busy straightening up her clothes and getting suitcases out of the way under the cots. "Why are you so interested in the cave?" she asked.

"I dunno."

"Now, Jeff—"

"I *heard* Dad, Mom! I'm not to go in alone."

"And don't go off anywhere else either without telling someone. Sometimes you're too impulsive for your own good."

I flipped over on my stomach, facing the net wall.

"Is something the matter?" Mom asked.

I closed my eyes.

"If you talk about it, maybe you'll find out things aren't as bad as they seem," she said.

Things were bad all right. Either she or Dad or Jen always managed to say something to let me know I had not lived down last year's troubles yet. I probably never would. . . . She and Dad did not trust me because one night last year I had left Jennifer by herself when they were gone for a couple of hours. They had depended on me to stay with her till they returned, but I had sneaked out. I didn't think Jennifer would even know I was gone but when I got back home and saw how frightened she was, it scared me too. Worst of all was the disappointment in Mom and Dad's eyes. The only thing Dad did was to put his arm across my shoulder and say, "I never thought you'd do something like this, Jeff."

I wish he had punished me instead.

Mom's voice broke into my memories. "Jeff, can't you talk—"

"No, I can't because you don't trust me!" I exploded.

Mom was silent a long time. When she spoke her soft voice seemed to blend with the cool breeze.

"The question isn't whether *we* trust you," she said.

"It's whether or not you trust yourself."

"Why didn't you say anything last year when I left Jennifer by herself?"

"Did we have to?"

"I would have known for sure how you felt."

49

"Didn't you?"

I did. That's what made me feel miserable. Would trusting myself make me feel better? I flopped over and looked at Mom.

She smiled. "You think about what I said."

"OK." I would think about it, but would it change anything? I took the pottery sherd from King Solomon's ancient city out of my pocket. I rubbed it against my cheek and felt its coolness and glazed smoothness. I would lie here the whole afternoon and *think*. How do I learn to trust myself? Anyway, who could sleep from one until four o'clock? That was for infants and tired grown-ups.

When I woke up and realized I had slept through the whole rest period, I was really disgusted. Now it was time for the late afternoon chores and I had not been thinking a bit.

I wished Kerim had been selected for my work team when the group was divided up. But he wasn't. The team I was on washed pottery which was found that day. It had been gathered into buckets according to area and field.

I liked the job of washing pottery best of all. Sometimes it was hard to clean so we used all sizes of brushes—from hand brushes down to tiny toothbrushes to scrub away the dirt. A piece completely crusted over with dirt would often turn out to be beautiful. I played guessing games to figure out what might be under the crust. Running my fingers over the clean sherds, I felt the lines of their design and traced the base rims of bowls and examined lips of vases with my fingers as well as my eyes.

Here in my own hand, I thought, is pottery someone made thousands of years ago. Perhaps it was someone like me or Kerim or Jennifer.

After we had washed the sherds, we laid each one out on the proper pile on straw mats to dry. Each pile came from the same location on the tell.

Jennifer finished her chore of picking up paper and other trash. She and Kerim were watching Mr. McDowell, Mr. Nebergall, and the other archaeologists. When I finished I joined them. Kerim nodded to me but said nothing.

The men were seated around a table "reading" the pottery which was already dry. They dated it—sometimes in a particular century, sometimes even a specific date. I eagerly watched their busy fingers. Mr. Mac especially, since he was the pottery expert, could "read" a whole pile in a few minutes.

The pottery which was not discarded was marked for identification and stored in labeled boxes for further study. From a few pieces a whole bowl or pitcher could be reconstructed in the laboratory in Jerusalem.

Kerim was on one of the teams putting the identifying marks on the sherds with India ink. His numbering was clear and even. I studied his brown hands while his fingers handled the pottery sherds as mine had done earlier to clean them. He glanced at me once.

"The cave," I whispered.

He went back to his work as if I didn't exist.

A "Dirt" Archaeologist

6

A "Dirt" Archaeologist

STREAKS OF RED AND LAVENDER RADIATED across the Mediterranean Sea. Mom said the sun arranged its spectacular exit—as if it hated to give up its power to the evening coolness. We gazed at the brilliant colors and listened to the evening lecture.

I knew better than to miss the lecture if I wanted a chance to "dig" rather than remain the errand boy. I learned that teams of archaeologists and volunteers like my parents had been working 10 or 12 summers to uncover this layer cake of history.

About halfway through Mr. Nebergall's slide show on the tell's history, I nudged Jennifer. "Hey, this helps me figure out the meaning to some of the stones and holes we saw today."

"Me too—a little," she said.

A layer of dung ash, for instance, indicated that fires had once been built on that spot. It was a ground level of some ancient time, and that time could be calculated by the experts. I wondered if the Bedouins at the base of the tell used animal dung for fire as our ancestors did?

Mr. Nebergall's slides included pictures of a burial site containing skeletons, pottery, coins, and jewelry; of walls and gates dating from various times in the city's history; and ancient altars of worship. A row of huge stones might have been altars erected at a gathering of several nomadic tribes. A small stone, probably used as an incense burner, was designed with a crude stick figure that was holding spears or lightning rods over his head.

"This figure may depict the god Baal," Mr. Nebergall explained. "Worship of the god Baal did take place here at various times. You will remember that the Israelites accused King Solomon in his old age of being too tolerant of those who worshiped idols. This stone may have been placed on a Baal altar."

The figure was similar to the ones on my sherd. But several figures—rather than only one—had been carved on my pottery piece, not holding spears but holding hands like paper doll cutouts. I punched Jennifer and whispered, "Are you sure you got this off the discard pile?"

"You can trust me."

Her answer hit a sore spot with me, so I punched her again.

"I'm gonna tell Mom!" she retorted.

"If you do—"

Dad put his hand on my shoulder.

"Dad says get quiet, Jennifer."

"I'm not talking!"

Dad's hand weighed heavier on my shoulder. Mr. Nebergall was still talking about Baal worship. While I listened I also wondered about my sherd. What if it had become a discard by mistake? I couldn't stand to give it up.

By the time the lecture was over, I could have slept on the bare rocks but I wasn't about to let anybody know it. And four o'clock was coming just as early tomorrow morning. I managed to brush my teeth and wash my face and hands at one of the sinks. I hung around listening to people talking for a while, then poked along slowly toward the rows of sleeping tents, glad that ours was nearby. It was getting dark, and the moon was rising. In the distance the lights of Tel Aviv sparkled like the stars overhead.

I could see Kerim walking home to the Bedouin camp. He looked so alone out there by himself. He passed all the black tents huddled close to the earth and entered the gate in the cactus enclosure. Inside where he lived it was dark—like the cave. I hoped he didn't bump noses with a camel. I also hoped his mother was waiting up for him.

57

When I crawled into my cot the dogs from the Bedouin camp were howling. A plane from a nearby air base roared overhead. In the quiet that followed, Dad suggested that we each think about what had impressed us on our first full day in the wilderness of Israel and each select a passage from the Bible to read aloud. I was always impatient at home when we read the Bible at the supper table, but here in the land where the Bible people lived, the writings seemed to come alive.

For my passage I should have selected "Honor thy father and mother" although I would have changed the word "honor" to "obey" because I kept having secret dreams about getting into the cave.

Instead, I read the 23rd Psalm of David because I would like nothing better than lying down beside still waters. Then I turned to my New Testament and read Jesus' words, "I am the bread of life; he who comes to Me shall not hunger, and he who believes in Me shall never thirst."

"I'm sunbaked on this dry land," I said to give my impression of our first day here. "And I'm never again going to take a drink of water for granted."

The next morning Dad suggested that I go to the cave with him after our second breakfast at 8:30. By seven o'clock I decided 8:30 would never arrive. To pass the time I delivered messages back and forth to field supervisors, carried tools, refilled *ibriks*. I even helped clean the latrines; at least *that* daily job was passed around among everyone. Back and forth across the tell I went. Each time I passed over the cave area, I walked along the rim and looked down the hillside at the entrance. I could not get a glimpse of Dad, Kerim, or anyone else.

I walked over and watched Hank break up some rocks with a pick.

"What's on your mind?" he asked.

"There's not going to be an 8:30 this morning," I replied.

"Maybe so." He pounded on a good-sized rock and split it. The largest piece tumbled over my way.

"Just throw it on the wheelbarrow to go to the dump," he said.

I picked it up. "Hey, look! There are deep grooves on four sides of this rock!"

Hank put his pick down and came over.

I said, "I think we ought to take it to Mr. Mac."

"Go ahead. Probably nothing to it."

I had heard Dad say you don't decide anything is worthless when you're digging, particularly if you aren't the expert. I lugged the huge rock a good city block back to the other end of the tell and deposited it on the "reading" table.

It turned out that the rock was a form for molding tools. Hot metal was poured into the mold,

Mr. Nebergall explained. A handle would be fit into it and held in place by a groove carved in rock. Two molds looked like chisels, another a spearhead.

"Young man, you have sharp eyes," Mr. McDowell said. "We are indebted to you that this did not go on the junk pile."

"Thank you, Sir." I was so excited I could hardly speak.

Mr. Mac pulled on his thick black beard. "I must admit, Jeff, that I had doubts about children as young as you and your sister being here on the dig. But I want you to know that we're glad you came with your parents." He didn't look stern at all now.

"Maybe I can be a 'dirt archaeologist' someday too," I said. I did not add that I hoped it would be soon.

I liked the way Mr. Mac laughed. It was as if we shared something special between us. I gazed long and hard once again at "my" rock and ran off to tell Hank and Mom and Jennifer. I watched where I was going this time and didn't fall sprawling over the wheelbarrows.

A Flicker of Light

7

A Flicker of Light

DON'T FORGET YOUR *IBRIK!*" Dad called. "You'll need it as much in the cave as up here in the sun."

I filled my *ibrik,* spilling some of our precious water in my haste. I ran ahead of Dad and as I started down the hillside, my foot slipped on some pebbles. I slid on my seat all the way to the bottom and came to a stop near the entrance to the cave.

"I didn't break it!" I yelled and held up the *ibrik* for Dad to see.

"Are *you* OK?"

"I think so." But sliding down the stair rail at home was more fun. I rubbed my sore seat.

"I'll lead the way," Dad said, flicking on his big flashlight.

The big mouth of the cave looked like it belonged to an angry giant. I entered the cave more cautiously than I had yesterday. I knew it curved away suddenly into pitch blackness. I shuddered when I lost the sun's direct rays.

"What's the matter, Jeff?" Dad asked. "You haven't been so quiet since we arrived."

"The cave seems to be telling me to shut up."

"We must walk quite a distance before we reach the burial places you saw in the pictures last night. Just because you can't see for miles doesn't mean you need to be jumpy about the underground. I won't run off and leave you," Dad said.

I knew that. After he had told me I couldn't enter alone, he wouldn't leave me for a second, I bet. Not that I wanted him to. I reached out and felt the sandy rock walls and felt a coolness seep into my skin. I could not tell Dad it was Kerim's strange behavior that made the cave seem mysterious. He would probably explain it all away, and I would be left with nothing. Whether the cave held something or nothing mysterious, I wanted to find that out for myself.

We made a turn to the left, and voices echoed through the cave. Sounds of shovels and brushes and scoops rolled out from the distance. Lantern light gleamed. Then we saw Dad's teammates already back at work. First Dad showed me the 15th and 14th century B. C. burial places which had been uncovered earlier in the summer.

"Where are the pottery and jewelry we saw in the pictures?" I asked.

"In Jerusalem. That Egyptian or Phoenician vase and the alabaster pedestal vase were beautiful after they were cleaned up, weren't they?"

Having scrubbed on sherds, I knew the hard work involved in getting to the beauty of those vases. "I just saw them in the picture," I said. "I wish I could have *felt* them."

Dad laughed. "I agree with you!"

He introduced me to Tim and Sally, a couple from a university in Tennessee.

"We've got tons of chunky debris to move out of here," Sally said. "You look like a good strong worker. You're hired!"

I glanced at Dad with hope.

He put his hand on my shoulder. "He's on a tour right now, Sally. Then he'll go back topside. He isn't 18, so you can't hire him unless Mr. Mac approves."

Sally mopped her forehead dramatically. "Even in the wilderness we have to fight the Establishment!"

Everybody laughed, and I asked why they must move so much rubble out. Tons sounded like an awful lot.

Sally grinned and winked at me. "We're going to find water in this here desert, if we have to dig to China."

"But Mr. Mac said there's a good year-round water supply."

Tim said, "What we're actually digging for is

more tombs which we believe are underneath us."

I studied the bones and skulls laid out on the burial mound. One tall figure and one small, perhaps a child, and lots of bones piled up in a corner as if they had been pushed aside to make room for the two stretched out. When I suggested that to Dad, he said I was exactly right.

My eyes were used to the dim light now and I gazed around in every direction from the small chamber that opened up from the passageway we had come through. There were goofer buckets, shovels, scoops and brushes of all sizes, and

screens—the same tools they had on top of the
tell. Everything looked quite ordinary. Suddenly
my blood felt like carbonated water racing
through my veins. Imagine the thought of a
3,500-year-old burial mound being ordinary!

Tim said, "Hello, Kerim. I need you."

I turned. Kerim passed me with a swift glance
in my direction.

"Hi!" I said.

"Hello." He wasn't too friendly. Maybe it was
because of the language barrier. Maybe.

"Kerim, you look pale. You're not getting

"You look like a good strong worker," said Sally.
"You're hired!"

enough sun," Sally said, as if he could understand her perfectly.

"I am fine, Miss Sally."

"Hey!" I exclaimed. "You *do* know English!"

"Only a little."

"A little, my hind foot! He knows *a lot*," Sally said. "He's just being modest."

"Please, Miss Sally."

"OK, I won't embarrass you, Kerim. But remember that he who runneth down himself will be runneth down by everybody!"

I laughed right out loud.

"I hate to mention it," one of the other workers said, "but we're getting nowhere fast."

"Come on, Jeff, I must get to work. I'll walk you back through the cave," Dad said. "Maybe you can come back another day."

"Right! I'm going to see about hiring you," Sally added.

"If you don't need the flashlight," I said to Dad, "why don't I just walk back by myself? If there was just one way in, then there's just one way out."

"Smart thinking there, Jeff!" That Sally was fun.

Just when I thought I might make Dad forget that I was not to walk in the cave alone, Kerim offered to walk back with me. I wondered why. There must be more to the cave than I had seen.

Kerim walked ahead with the flashlight,

surefooted as one who had walked the path many times. I wanted to ask him why he had stuffed food in his pockets yesterday, but I didn't dare. He was silent and so was I. Here was my chance to talk with him alone and I muffed it. His straight back looked forbidding.

We turned to the right. "Uh, Kerim, uh, did I see all of the cave?"

There was a long silence. Finally he answered, "I do not know what you saw."

I was tired of his little games—pretending he could not understand me yesterday, keeping me out of the cave, being shifty about answering my question.

"For Pete's sake, we walked down this way from the entrance and ended up where you are all working. And all I want to know is if there're any other parts to this cave?"

He shrugged. "Who knows?"

"I bet you do!"

He said nothing.

"The entrance is to the right," he said finally.

I saw only black nothingness ahead and stared into it. He stepped aside and motioned for me to pass.

"You turn right here and you will see light from the day."

I stepped forward where the cave curved to the entrance. Its yawning mouth was bright now instead of dark. For some reason I didn't want to walk toward it and have to admit to myself that the cave was just a plain ordinary cave and that its only mysteries were thousands of years old. So I looked across from where we stood. If we had turned right instead of curving left when we entered the cave, where would it have taken us?

I blinked. Had I imagined a pinpoint of light in that direction? Now there was only midnight blackness. I blinked again and this time there could be no mistake. A tiny flicker of light rose and faded in an instant.

I turned and stared at Kerim but I kept silent. Suddenly I was afraid to say anything.

Jeff's Discovery

8

Jeff's Discovery

KERIM WAS SHAKING HIS HEAD. I guessed he meant for me to be quiet. I felt in my pants pocket for my sherd and held it tightly.

I finally found my voice; it had become a whisper. "Are—are you coming outside with me?"

He shook his head again. "You do not need me. I wait here for you to leave. Then I return to work with my team."

His voice sounded pretty normal. Maybe he did not see the flicker of light.

"Go now. We have much work to do."

"Tell my father that I didn't go anywhere by myself," I said. Suddenly I wanted very much to talk with Dad.

"Of course you obey your father. Every boy obeys his father."

That was a help. It sounded as definite as an umpire's decision.

"See you!" I said and ran toward the light.

The sun about struck me down. My *ibrik* of water! I had left it in the cave. I stood in the entrance and wondered what to do. Should I go back to the curve and call Kerim? But whatever caused that flicker of light might hear me. Why not go back? I wouldn't be so far behind Kerim that I could not see by his light. I tiptoed back to the curve and looked down the passageway. I saw nothing. How could Kerim have gone down that long passageway so quickly? No flicker showed up behind me to the right of the entrance. Had I been seeing things? I blinked but saw nothing. I ran back to the sunlight, then pulled off my shirt, wiped my face with it, and tied it around my waist.

When I turned and glanced up the side of the tell, I saw Jennifer sitting on the top waving at me.

"I'm waiting for you," she called.

Nosy. I climbed the hill and lay down on my stomach on top of the tell, covering my face in the crook of my elbow.

"What happened, huh? What'd you do? What'd you see? Come on, Jeff—"

"Will you leave me alone, please?"

"Just for that you don't get any of my water!" She hugged her *ibrik*.

"Don't threaten!" It felt really good to be fuss-

74

ing with Jennifer after my scare in the cave. Safe, that's how it felt.

"Why did you come outside twice?" she asked.

"Quit bugging me."

"Why?"

"So I can think!"

"Wow! Imagine that!"

The rocky ground began to hurt. I sat up and brushed off my chest and stomach. "Jennifer, do you want to go in the cave?"

"We don't have a flashlight. Anyway, I'm scared."

"There's nothing to be scared of, I tell you." I was telling myself too.

"I'm scared of the dark."

"Since when?"

"Since right now!"

Somebody was calling my name. It was Mr. Mac. Jennifer tagged right along with me.

"We need you to fill *ibriks,* Jeff. You can help, Jennifer. And Area Two needs another goofer bucket and hand trowel."

For the rest of the morning I didn't have a minute to myself. When Kerim brought my *ibrik* to me at lunch, he acted as if he didn't even know me.

I tried to put the cave out of my mind. The tiny flicker of light I had seen in the dark just before I came back to the exit kept tempting me. Kerim's definite "Every boy obeys his father" didn't sound so final anymore. It sounded as if you could always know what was right and what was wrong. I didn't believe that. There were many times when I didn't know what was right or wrong, and I tried to convince myself this was one of them. The cave was perfectly safe for human travel; what would be wrong with my turning to the right inside the entrance and following the flicker?

But Dad had said in his most stern voice that I was not to go in alone, so that made it wrong, I guess. If I wanted Mom and Dad to trust me, maybe I should scout around and see if I could find someone else to help me explore. Still, I wanted to find out for myself. The idea of finding someone to go with me put a terrible taste in my mouth, like much too much salt on a boiled egg.

All that day and the next went by while I tried to decide what to do. Now I was hunting for a cave plan and a counter cave plan.

The next morning Mr. McDowell came up to me at the second breakfast. "I've been watching you, Jeff," he said.

My chest got all tight. I had not gone back again to the cave alone, but I wondered if he could read my thoughts.

He pulled on his beard. "You're quite careful when you wash pottery every afternoon; you have a keen, sharp eye. The result of that is this marvelous example of a tool mold. Would you like to try your hand as a 'dirt' archaeologist this morning?"

"Oh, boy! Would I!"

"Come with me."

I followed him to the opposite end of the tell where the wall of one of Solomon's cities had been uncovered. I wanted to run all the way but decided that would not be proper for someone who was just promoted.

"We're trying to get to bedrock down the side of this wall," he said. "Do you know Chris? You'll be working with him and Hank."

Hank. The baggy-eyed one who almost tossed away the tool mold.

Chris told me we were going to use hand trowels now and move slowly. If we were to find anything, we would not want to ruin it with a shovel or pick. I was so excited I did not even mind how long it took us. Every few inches Hank took measurements and Chris wrote them in a book. Volunteers in other squares were finding pitchers and metal blades, but we found nothing important. I would be happy with *anything*.

"You're too impatient," Dad said later in our tent.

I pulled up a second blanket as the cool night breezes moved in from the sea.

"I'll be disappointed if I don't turn up anything," I said drowsily and went to sleep without dreaming about the cave.

The next morning as we dug deeper down the side of the ancient city wall, it got hotter and hotter. The tell's ground level was now over my head.

"We're digging ourselves into an oven," Hank complained.

I kept brushing with a medium-sized brush across the surface of our square area as if I knew my discovery was coming. I uncovered a grayish black layer. I rubbed my hand lightly over the grainy surface. Excitement rippled through me when I recognized what it was.

"Dung ash!" I yelled. "Three thousand years old! Isn't it *beautiful*?"

Everybody around me laughed. I did too. I would be satisfied to find *anything* at all, I had said.

While Chris measured and noted my dis overy, I could just see a real live mother like mine or Kerim's, only from a long time ago, who tended this fire for those she loved.

Love Energy

9

Love Energy

THE NEXT DAY WAS FRIDAY. I was looking forward to two things: Dad had said I could go back to the cave that morning—Sally had convinced Mr. McDowell they could use me—and we were leaving that afternoon for a trip, since the weekends were free for travel.

Kerim fell into step beside me on the way to the cave after our peanut butter sandwich breakfast. I wondered why.

Jennifer ran up and grabbed my hand. "I'll miss you, Jeff, but you'll tell me all about it, won't you?"

"Don't get mushy!"

"Quit pulling away. I have something to give you."

I stopped and patiently waited (Dad would have been proud) and said: "What?"

She still held onto my hand. "Do you remember last year when we hiked in the desert mountains in California?"

"So what?"

"You remember how tired we got and you lay down on the desert sand and said you were dying—and how Mom squeezed our hands and said she was passing love energy to us—and how it made us laugh and not feel so tired anymore?"

"Yeah, I remember." I would never forget it.

Jennifer's big brown eyes stared up at me. "I'm just passing you some love energy, Jeff, to get you past the dark down there."

I squeezed her hand in return. "I'll tell you about the cave," I promised.

"Your sister I like," Kerim said as we walked down the hill.

Right now I did too. "Do you have sisters?"

He shook his head. "No, only two brothers. My baby sister died."

"I'm sorry."

"No, it was best. Believe me, it was best."

"Kerim, do you like this work?"

His dark eyes seemed to catch fire. "Oh, yes. I like very much."

When I asked him if he wanted to be an archaeologist someday, he said his father was only a poor Bedouin. "And I have little school. We move by the seasons to the best water supply."

"When will you leave here?"

He shrugged. "My father says perhaps we stay. He finds work in the rich valley. My brothers and I work on the tell in the spring and summer. So if we stay, one day I may go to school. But archaeologist? Oh, I would like. But no—I am afraid it is not for me."

Inside the entrance to the cave I turned to him impulsively and said, "We're going to the Sea of Galilee this weekend. Could you go with us?"

He stood dead still. "Do you mean it?"

"Of course."

"I must ask my father." He smiled for the first time since I had met him. "I think you must also ask your father."

"I will when we catch up with him. Hold that light steady, Kerim. To tell the truth, I'm a little uneasy in here—nothing tough, you know—but I keep seeing things in the blackness. In fact, the other day I thought I saw a light—"

Kerim clapped his hand over my mouth. I lost my balance and fell backward to the ground. Before I could yell at him, he was helping me up.

"You saw nothing!" he whispered fiercely.

Then in a normal voice—a monotone in fact—he said, "Forgive me. I did not mean—"

"That's OK." I brushed my clothes. "It took me by surprise and I lost my balance—that's all."

"What took you by surprise, Jeff?"

Just when I thought I was beginning to know him a little, he came up with a strange remark again. I was churning inside; he had given himself away even if I didn't know why. He knew something about this cave, and I was going to find it out if it took me the whole month.

"Did you answer me, Jeff?"

I was not good at instant answers. Finally I said, "I guess I just got whammied by Jennifer's love energy."

"Yes, I understand."

"I don't!"

"Let us hurry. Miss Sally is waiting for us."

I hoped Dad was also waiting for us.

I felt jittery. Sally's teasing got on my nerves, as Mom says. I finally went over to Kerim and asked, "Why did you act so funny at the entrance?"

"I do not know what you mean."

Didn't he trust me either? Was that why he would not tell me what his strange behavior was all about? If he didn't trust me enough to tell me, I wasn't sure I wanted him to go with us for the weekend.

"You're doing a great shoveling job, Jeff. You're watching carefully and that's important," Sally said. "Say, where did you learn to shovel so well?"

Real funny. I didn't bother to answer. In a few minutes Dad moved over near me.

"It's nice to have you on our team today, Jeff."

Did I look so glum that they had to give me a

buildup? I set aside my shovel and hunted my *ibrik*; I offered it to Dad. While he drank I half-heartedly asked if Kerim could go with us on the weekend. I realized I couldn't back out after mentioning it to him. Next time I wouldn't be so quick to offer.

Dad glanced at Kerim. I could tell he was listening.

"Of course," Dad said. "When can you ask your parents, Kerim?"

"Tonight, Sir, when you are eating."

"Good! We want to leave right after dinner on the bus that's coming out to take some of us to Jerusalem. Tell your father we're going on up to the Sea of Galilee, and we'll take good care of you."

"Oh, thank you. Never in my life have I gone to Galilee."

"Neither have we," Dad said, "so we'll discover it together."

The Sign of the Fish

10

The Sign of the Fish

IT WAS NOT JUST BECAUSE OUR TELL was on the
edge of the desert. In fact, the rich plain below the
tell would not be rich without irrigation. It could
not have been because we sometimes ached to
shower for hours or splash in puddles. It could not
have been these things that made me know the
minute I saw the Lake of Galilee why Jesus had
spent so much time there.

There was no breeze to wipe away the burning
heat from our faces, but the heat did not matter as
I gazed at the rich blue water and the Jordanian
hills that rose in the distance across the lake.
Once the lake had come into view, Jennifer and I
had convinced Dad to stop as often as possible.
Each time we waded with Kerim on the shore and
felt the coolness of all that water on our feet.

It was a long day's journey before we arrived in

Capernaum after spending Friday night in Jerusalem. We had left very early in a rented car—one which Dad had arranged for through a Christian because all Jewish businesses were closed for the Sabbath.

We were there at last, walking along the shore and splashing in the shallow water and exploring the ruins of the ancient Capernaum synagogue a hundred yards away.

"This was Peter and James and John's hometown," Mom said.

It seemed strange to call this place a town when only limestone blocks and a few Corinthian columns of the synagogue remained.

I hated to leave the shore to explore the ruins, but when Dad began to talk about the synagogue remains uncovered only about 65 years ago but dating from about A. D. 200, I got excited.

"See how the blocks of native black basalt contrast sharply with the imported white limestone blocks of the synagogue," Dad pointed out.

"What about these?" I asked.

"That may well be the foundation of the first-century synagogue, the one Jesus would have preached in. You know, He began His ministry here." Dad's excitement rubbed off on me and evidently on Kerim, too.

I had been wondering all day if Kerim, since he was probably a Muslim, had been disgusted with so much talk about Christian and Jewish history.

90

I hoped not. Maybe I would get a chance this weekend to ask him about his faith. I wanted to know more about Muslims since Jerusalem was their holy city, too.

Now he was asking Dad a question. "Why did Jesus choose Capernaum to begin His work?"

"It may always be a mystery, Kerim," Dad said. "Capernaum was certainly an important city in Jesus' day, and most of His ministry was in the province of Galilee. I would like to know the answer to that question, too. It may lie somewhere in the remains along this shore—those not yet uncovered."

"What do you mean?"

"Just that the ancient city probably covered a mile or more along the lakeshore."

"Why hasn't it all been excavated?"

"Lack of people, money, and time, Jeff. There are centuries of archaeological work ahead."

I liked that idea. His words stirred my mind and I turned to gaze at the harp-shaped lake, called Kinneret from the Hebrew word for harp.

"I found a Star of David!" Jennifer called. It was sculptured in the white limestone.

Kerim was moving his hand over the black basalt of the earliest remains. "It feels different from the limestone," he said.

"Me-ow!"

It was the softest sound, but unmistakable. "I heard a kitten!" I exclaimed.

Nobody believed me.

"Sh!" I moved in what I thought was the direction of the sound, and then I saw a tiny black something running in the opposite direction. I dashed over the ruins and turned a corner in time to see it disappear down a hole in the side of a wall. Calling for help, I started scratching at the hard dry earth.

"That kitten—it has to be a kitten—ran down this hole. I can't see anything. I can't reach my hand any farther than *that*. Oh, for a pick or shovel!"

Dad said the animal—whatever it was—might be half a mile away by now. I said it must be in that hole. I kept digging. Jennifer and Kerim helped—all three of us on our knees scrabbling, with little results. Kerim found a stone with a sharp point to break away the dirt.

"I feel something furry! Maybe I have its tail!"

Kerim's stone made a pinging sound.

"Oh!"

When I saw what Kerim was holding, I jumped up, forgetting that I had *something* by its tail. I yanked out of the hole a screeching black kitten. He hissed and pawed, but when I stuck him in the crook of my arm he quieted down as if he thought he was back inside the hole.

Mom and Dad and Jennifer and Kerim were examining the piece of pottery he had uncovered.

"I saw a fish carved on it!" I said.

Dad held Kerim's outstretched hand which contained the pottery nestled in his palm. Dad couldn't take his eyes off it. Finally he said in a breathless voice, "Let's go wash off the dirt."

The kitten scratched my side, so I rubbed its back to calm it.

On the way to the lake we talked about how sign of a fish became an identifying mark of a Christian.

"Why?" Jennifer asked.

"Because a lot of Jesus' followers were fishermen, and He asked them to drop their nets and become fishers of men," I said, proudly remembering a Sunday school lesson from last spring.

"Why did they need a sign? Why didn't they just *tell* each other they were Christian?"

"Get this, Jennifer, if you were being persecuted for being a Christian, would you go shouting it around? No! You'd draw a fish on the ground and if the stranger were a Christian, he would draw one back. If he weren't, he wouldn't understand what it meant. Is that clear?"

"But, Jeff, why a fish? Why not a bird?"

"I just told you." Jennifer had a way of asking just enough questions to pull out of me everything I knew about it.

"Maybe I can make it clearer," Dad said. "It was much later after Jesus' death and resurrection that Christians were punished more and more for worshiping Him. They believed He was

"There's a fish on it!"

'Jesus Christ, Son of God, Savior.' And the first letters of each of those words in the Greek language spell *FISH*. So the sign of the fish meant that that person believed Jesus was the Christ, Son of God, Savior."

"Wow, that was like a secret code!"

"They needed one, Jen, for their own safety sometimes."

"I should say so! I wouldn't want to be prosecuted—uh, persecuted—whatever that means!"

We all squatted at the water's edge and watched Kerim dip the pottery sherd into the water. While he scrubbed it with his fingers, Dad told us how some first-century fishermen's huts had been unearthed around the Sea of Galilee, where lamps were found with Christian signs of fish, lambs, or crosses in their designs.

"Those signs are all over our church," Jennifer said. "Now I know why—a little bit."

I held the black furry ball of kitten down for a drink but he drew his head into my cupped hands.

"This sherd may be very significant," Dad said.

Mom laughed shakily. "After this experience, you'll never get the archaeology bug out of your system."

"Never!" Dad said emphatically.

"It *is* a fish!" Kerim said.

Dad took his handkerchief out of his pocket, and Kerim wrapped it around the piece of pottery.

Mom emptied a small purse inside her large purse (her "walking suitcase," Dad called it), and Kerim placed it inside, almost reverently I thought.

"We'll take it to Mac and let him evaluate it," Dad said.

While the kitten snuggled down in the tail of my T-shirt, we sat on the sand and listened to Dad tell about Jesus healing the centurion's servant at Capernaum. A sudden strong wind picked up the water in leaping waves. I remembered the story of how Jesus calmed those waters for frightened fishermen caught in their boat. The breeze was like cold water washing the heat from my face.

The fish on the sherd, Dad's excited voice retelling a familiar story, the wind whipping up the waves—all these made me feel that Jesus must have thought this was the most beautiful lake in the world! I absently drew a fish design in the sand with my toes, remembering our conversation about how the early followers of Jesus had identified themselves to one another with such a sign.

I felt the sudden sensation of someone staring at me and glanced up. Kerim's dark eyes looked straight into mine as he carefully drew the shape of a fish in the sand at his feet.

"You Must Trust Me"

11

"You Must Trust Me"

THAT MOMENT WAS OURS TO KEEP FOREVER.
Neither of us spoke, but we both rose and walked
together along the shore. I could not explain my
happiness over his being a Christian—it was the
way he had told me with the sign of the fish, as if
we were living back in Jesus' day. There was no
need to speak.

I did not know how long we had been walking
when Kerim said, "About the cave—you must
trust me, Jeff. That is all I can say."

I did not answer immediately.

"I'll trust you, Kerim."

It would have been much easier if he had
shared more, but maybe he didn't know how.
After all his strange actions and conversations, I
was surprised at myself that I could give up all
my suspicions just because of two fish scrawled in

the sand. Was this how the followers of Jesus had felt long ago? Suddenly I felt very close to them.

We returned to Mom and Dad and Jennifer. Dad put one hand on my shoulder and one on Kerim's.

We drove south along the Sea of Galilee and spent the night at Tiberias, a town right on the shore that was built, Dad said, by Herod Antipas, son of Herod the Great, in the first century A. D. and named in honor of the Roman Emperor Tiberius.

There were hot sulphur springs here, Dad said, in what I called his teacher-happy voice over passing on his knowledge to someone else. He went into detail about the town's history, but I lost him. I was more interested in looking at the buildings and watching the people on the streets. Tiberias was a nice mixture of ancient and modern.

In the cool evening breezes we walked along the seashore; we could not stay away from the water. Sailboats were anchored in the shallows, and lights from the dwellings twinkled like stars.

Stories from the Gospels came alive because we were walking in the land where Jesus and His disciples had walked. Now as we walked along the shore at Tiberias, we recalled stories about Jesus and wondered where they occurred. Once Mom laughed and said: "We sound like we're remembering experiences that happened to us personally."

"That's the way it is with Jewish-Christian tradition," Dad said solemnly. "Their experience long ago 'happens' to us, too, because we're linked to them through faith."

I would have to think about that for a while. I gazed out across the dark water. The Sea of Galilee, or Lake Kinneret, as the Israelis called it. I liked the musical rhythm of the Hebrew word *Kinneret*.

"Kinneret," I said. "The harp lake. I like that, Mom."

"I like Sea of Galilee best," said Jennifer, stroking Something, the name we had given the kitten.

Kerim joined in. "I like them both. The name does not change the lake, does it?"

Kerim was not more than a couple of years older than I, but he seemed so wise. I wished I could be wise. Sometimes one little remark of his would bring out the meaning of whatever we were seeing or talking about.

Dad said we must tear ourselves away from the water and get back to our rooms, for a big day with a long drive was ahead of us the next day. As we walked back to the hotel, I remembered the conversation with Kerim at Capernaum. I hardly knew him and yet I promised I would trust him.

Early the next morning after breakfast, I went

out on the roof of the dwelling we had stayed in during the night. It was fun to look across the lake to the Jordanian hills on the other side, up and down the beautiful lakeshore, and over the whole town of Tiberias. Few people were out on the streets.

I was surprised to see Kerim walking down the street below me which ran in front of the hotel. Where was he going? I started to call to him and wave, but he was almost to the corner. Suddenly a young man—an Arab with a white headdress held in place with a black braid rope—came flying around the corner. He ran smack into Kerim. They each looked as if they were apologizing and going their way; then they stopped and stared.

Kerim tried to run, but the stranger grabbed him by the collar. He talked intensely while he kept his stranglehold on Kerim's collar.

"Hey!" I screeched, then jumped up and down and waved my arms.

Kerim and the stranger jerked around.

"Here I am, Kerim! On the roof!"

Kerim pulled away and ran toward our hotel while the Arab dashed around the corner and disappeared out of sight. I struck out for ground level and met Kerim at the entrance.

"Are you all right?"

*Kerim tried to run, but the stranger
grabbed him by the collar.*

"Come with me!" He wouldn't let me say anything until we were safe in our room.

"Are you all right?" I repeated.

"Yes—yes." He seemed a little angry at my question.

"Well, that man. Who was he?"

"I do not know."

"But he acted like he knew you. And you!" I stared hard at him. "You looked like you recognized him too."

"You must believe me. I do not *know* him!"

"I'll believe you, but it sure is hard. Have you ever seen him?"

Kerim walked over to a small table in the corner and put his hand on Dad's Bible. He then returned and stood directly in front of me. "I asked you yesterday to trust me, Jeff. Will you now make another promise to me?"

"I guess so."

"Please do not mention to anyone what just happened. It is our secret. Will you agree?"

"You must have a reason." Maybe he would tell me.

"Yes, I have a reason. And one more promise?"

His dark eyes were almost slate-colored in the room's dim light. He had really been frightened; he couldn't hide that from me.

I nodded.

"If you ever find somewhere a drawing of a fish—" he paused.

I nodded again, my throat suddenly tight.

"You will know by it that danger is near."

"What must I do?"

"You must get help at once, and you must find me."

"Do you mean *you* are in danger?"

"I do not know. I want a signal with you. That's all."

"S-sure, Kerim. But—but if you feel that way, maybe you better not go off by yourself like you did just now."

"I do not intend to."

He sat down on a cot. I sat on another one, feeling sick to my stomach.

We waited for my parents to return from breakfast.

We explored the archaeological excavations out on the mound in Tiberias, believed to be the ruins of the Biblical city of Hammath (which means "hot-spring," for the healing hot sulphur springs, Dad told us). Ruins of a fourth-century A. D. synagogue contained a beautiful mosaic floor. But I was not interested in any of it. I could not get my mind off Kerim and his encounter in the morning with the Arab. I kept trying to figure out for myself who the man might have been. He had looked pretty young. And how did Kerim know anybody in Tiberias?

A fish—"danger is near," Kerim had said. Did

the cave back at our tell have anything to do with this danger?

I shivered when I saw a troop of Israeli youth march in the street. "They're part of a military training program," Mom said.

"They don't look old enough to be soldiers," Jennifer said.

"Their country is in danger. All Israelis are obligated to protect it."

Danger.

"Is that because the Arabs want their land back?"

"Partly, Jennifer. But it's much more complicated than that."

Dad glanced at his watch. "We must leave now if we are to get back to Jerusalem in time to catch our bus to the tell."

I hated to leave the harp-shaped lake, Galilee. But I think Kerim was as relieved as I was that we got away from Tiberias without seeing the Arab again.

Distant Gunfire

12

Distant Gunfire

WHEN WE RETURNED TO THE TELL everything was different. In the first place, we could hear gunfire in the distance. A few volunteers had talked about limited guerrilla fighting by the Arab Palestinians earlier in the summer, but we had seen none of it since we arrived. I had never heard real guns before.

"I'm scared!"

"You're just a baby, Jennifer. Why don't you be strong like the Israeli kids? They didn't get the name *sabra* for nothing." But I was scared too.

"What's that mean?"

"A *sabra* is a cactus, Jen," Mom said quietly. "A kind that is all prickly on the outside, but the fruit inside is very sweet."

Dad added, "*Sabra* also means a hedge of thorns."

"You mean the kids are like a thorn hedge or a cactus? I don't get it!"

"It's a symbolic meaning, sweetheart—that is, they're good defenders, they adapt well to the sunbaked land—"

"I wouldn't like to be called a cactus!" Jennifer said.

"You would if you were sweet inside!"

Mom reproved me with a stiff glance.

"I must go home," Kerim said. He thanked my father and mother for the trip. He shook Jennifer's hand and gripped mine.

"Remember!" he whispered cautiously.

I nodded. My stomach tightened up like a dried apricot. "Are you sure you'll be safe? Don't you want us to walk home with you?"

"No, it is not far. I will go alone."

Jennifer, who had latched onto our kitten all afternoon, held it out gently. "You take Something with you for company and bring him back tomorrow."

He stroked the kitten on the head. "Please keep her with you. I have a brown one at home who sleeps with me every night."

Jennifer smiled. "I'm glad you told me. But if you need Something anytime, you'll ask, won't you?"

"Yes, I'll ask."

"Kerim, it was our pleasure to have you, and I will stand here and watch you walk across the

110

plain," Dad said. "Please tell your father thank you for sharing you with us this weekend."

Kerim's smile spread all over his face. Then he ran down the hillside. It was twilight, and gunfire echoed against the mountains. I stood with Dad until Kerim was safe inside the Bedouin camp.

Most of the tell's volunteers came from the United States with a few from other countries. We all acted jittery. Everyone was talking about the past war, the Palestinian guerrillas, and didn't the guns sound closer now?

The Israelis and Arabs in the group did not pay much attention. They were concerned but they were also used to guerrilla outbreaks, they said; it was a part of living here. No guerrillas had come as far into the interior as the tell (since most of the shelling was on the borders), so everyone could calm down and go about business as usual. It did not pay to go out looking for trouble, Mr. Nebergall said, and particularly where guerrillas were concerned. They could be anywhere—like grasshoppers in the fields. One just learned to live as if his enemy were miles away—or next door.

"I want to know why there's fighting," Jennifer demanded. "Nobody here has enemies; at least, I sure don't."

Mr. McDowell set Jennifer on his knee. "How about a lesson on Israel's history?"

"Okay."

I needed it too, but this would be a good time to show my pottery sherd to one of the archaeologists to be sure it was okay for me to keep it. I couldn't bear to think of giving it up, but I didn't want to keep it if it was valuable to the work on the tell. Besides, I wanted to get my mind off guns and guerrillas and anything else that had made the tell so different over the weekend.

I dug the sherd out of my pocket and took it to Mr. Nebergall.

"Son, you look sick."

"Yes, Sir. I mean, my sister found this on the discard pile. She gave it to me our first day here."

"What do you want to know about it?"

"I want to know if it got on the discard pile by mistake."

He took the piece and handled it carefully, lovingly almost. He looked at me as if he were trying to make up his mind about what to say or how to break the news to me.

"Is that all you wanted to know about it?"

"Yes, Sir, it is. I know you could tell me a lot more—probably date it. It's quite old, isn't it?"

He grinned. "A few thousand."

"And you could explain the stick figures—"

"Maybe."

"And you could explain the sun—isn't it a sun glaring down on the figures?"

He turned it this way and that. "Is that what you believe?"

"Yes. And you could tell me about the glaze but—but—"

"But what?" He seemed very patient.

"But I don't really want you to. I want to put my own meaning to it, don't you see? And I want to 'read' it for myself someday. I want to know enough someday to date it myself—and all those other things you do when you read pottery."

"Do you really?"

"Yes, I do." I stood up straight and took a deep breath, surprising myself at all that I was admitting.

"This piece means a great deal to you."

"Yes."

He motioned me to a table where we washed pottery late every afternoon. I sat on a bench beside him.

"I want to show you something." His long fingers rubbed the sherd. He showed me its curve and traced the lip of the piece and then the opposite edge where a rim or base was located on one corner. He showed me how, with some indication of the base and the lip, I could follow out the curve's measurement and reconstruct a bowl the exact size of the original.

"You must come to the laboratory if you are in Jerusalem next weekend," he said. "You will be able to see some of our workers actually reconstructing pots or bowls or vases from such a beginning as this piece."

"Could we visit?"

"Of course."

"Then this must be a valuable piece."

"Yes," he admitted. "It is most valuable to you. I can see into your future, I think, and I believe you are going to reconstruct that bowl—and perhaps not too long from now. How old are you, Jeff?"

"I'm 12, going on 13." I added, "going on 13," like my mother does when she wakes me at 4:05 and says it's "going on 5:00."

Mr. Nebergall placed the sherd gently into my palm. He said, "Jewish boys have a religious ceremony, a bar mitzvah, when they're 13 to celebrate their coming to manhood."

"At 13 years old?"

He nodded, still holding my hand with the sherd in it.

"Bar mitzvahs are beautiful. So is this sherd. And it is yours because it was given to you and because you accepted it. You're discovering many things on the tell, Jeff, and I'm confident that one day you'll be able to 'read' this gift for yourself."

"Oh, thank you, Sir." Words seemed so inadequate. I figured, though, that Mr. Nebergall knew exactly how I felt.

When I passed them, Mr. Mac was still trying to explain to Jennifer why fighting erupted regularly in Israel. For a few minutes I had forgotten all about it. But now I heard some distant firing.

I went off to the showers and then got ready for bed. I wanted time to think about my sherd and my dreams I had shared with Mr. Nebergall, and to think about Kerim and all that had happened during the weekend.

But mostly I wanted the comfort of my own sleeping bag to blot out the flares against the dark skies and the gunfire in the distance.

Kerim's Sherd

13

Kerim's Sherd

I WOKE UP WITH AN UNEASY FEELING the next morning before the alarm jangled. Mom and Dad were already stirring around, but I snuggled back under the covers to listen for sounds of shelling. Guerrilla raids were sporadic, Dad had said last night, and probably would be over almost as quickly as they had come.

I didn't hear anyone talk about last night's gunfire at breakfast, but there was none of the laughing and joking that usually went on in the dining shed. The silence was difficult to live with, too, I discovered.

After we finished eating, Dad motioned for all of us and Kerim to stay with him. He wanted us in on the conversation with Mr. McDowell, the pottery expert, about the sherd with the fish sign which Kerim had found at Capernaum.

When he heard that we had been to Capernaum on the weekend, Mr. Mac pounded us kids with questions. Did we see all the rich sculptures in the ruins—palm trees, clusters of grapes, and the seven-branched candelabrum? We nodded and added the Star of David to his list.

Dad said, "I think they went over those synagogue ruins with a fine-tooth comb. Kerim uncovered this when they dug a hole to rescue a kitten."

Mr. Mac held the piece as carefully as Mr. Nebergall had held mine last night.

"Beautiful! Beautiful!" He asked us to tell him exactly how we found it. He then got a small box and laid the piece inside.

"What are you doing with it?" Jennifer demanded.

"We'll label this box so that the sherd is identified as thoroughly as possible. Then it'll go to the laboratory in Jerusalem."

"But it belongs to Kerim!"

"Now what would we archaeologists do, Jennifer, if everyone who happened on a find such as this kept it to himself? We wouldn't discover nearly as much about our heritage, would we?"

"I guess not."

"Do you think it's first century?" I asked.

"No. I would say early third century. Pottery with many Christian motifs—such as the fish, lamb, cross—has been found in Galilee."

"Then you don't really need this sherd." Jennifer still sounded worried.

"That all depends. Usually loose pieces found on top of the ground aren't important because they aren't related to any particular earth stratum. That makes accurate dating more difficult."

"But we—I mean Kerim—didn't find this on top of the ground."

Mr. Mac nodded. "That's the reason it's going to the lab."

"What if you decide to discard it?" I asked.

"I doubt that will happen. But we'll put Kerim's name on it, and if it isn't kept we'll return it to him."

Jennifer went over and stood beside Kerim. "That's better," she said. "I hope the sherd isn't important."

"It already is important to me," said Kerim softly.

Mr. McDowell summoned the team photographer to take pictures of the sherd Kerim had found and the one Jennifer had given to me from the discard pile. I was pleased that they were taking pictures of them together and asked the photographer to give us copies of the photos. Kerim's sherd then went back into the box, properly labeled, and mine back into my pocket.

We grabbed our *ibriks* when Dad said it was time to get to work. I was glad Jennifer was going into the cave with Dad and me since Mom could not look after her down in her trench.

It was going to be another hot day—bright and beautiful with a blue sky above, streaked only with jet streams. As we headed down the hill to the cave entrance, I gazed off toward the Mediterranean Sea. Tel Aviv, 15 miles away on the coast, was in clear view. The radio, Dad said, had reported this morning some guerrilla activity near Tel Aviv. I decided that 15 miles away was too close.

It was obvious why our tell had been such an important location for a city. An enemy would have a hard time approaching it because the view was unlimited from the tell in three directions. To the west lay the plains and Tel Aviv on the coast. North one could follow the Mediterranean coastline all the way to the hills of Judah, and to the south as far as Ashkelon. The mountains were right upon us to the east. Two major roads crossed on the plains between us and the sea, and since the ancient border of Egypt was not far away to the south, the roads carried trade and armies within a few miles.

I could stare over the plain and almost see the armies of the pharaohs and of Saul and Solomon and David pass by.

When we arrived at the section of the cave being excavated, Sally and Tim and others were hard at work. I worked near Dad and asked him to tell Jennifer and Kerim and me more about the city's history. I had forgotten some of it from the evening lectures, and I especially needed it to take my mind off the tension around us. Dad retraced how the city had been conquered by the Egyptians off and on between 2,000 and 1,200 B.C., that it was a Philistine city for several hundred years, that King David had engaged its Canaanite peoples in battle many times, but it became a part of Israel when the pharaoh of Egypt gave it to King Solomon, when his daughter became Solomon's wife.

"It was a strong city for hundreds and hundreds of years—an excellent location with fertile valleys and a year-round water supply. What more could it need?" Dad asked.

A shade tree, I thought.

Dad continued, "And it didn't die out permanently until the first century A.D."

"Then people were living here when Jesus lived?"

"Yes, but we have no record that Jesus ever passed this way during His ministry."

"This place has been dead 1900 years!"

"Until our archaeology teams came 12 or more years ago," Dad added. "Now it's very much alive—at least every spring and summer."

I shuddered to think this city and plain were the locations of so much warfare in ancient times.

I asked Dad anxiously, "Does history often repeat its bad mistakes?"

Dad went on filling his goofer bucket with debris. "I'm afraid so, Son. I'm afraid so."

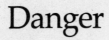

Danger

14

Danger

AT LUNCH MOM BROUGHT ME a large round stone. "For your slingshot, Jeff."

She wasn't joking, I found out, when Mr. Mac explained that it was used in ancient times as a slingstone. My fingers could barely reach around it.

I dropped it into Jennifer's hand, and it caught her off balance.

"Is that ever heavy! Wow!" She returned it to me.

Mr. Mac said, "We've found enough of these around the old fortress wall to fill several buckets, so you may keep this one."

"Let's see you carry *that* in your pocket!"

"Worry about your own pockets, Jen!" I said and then could have bitten my tongue for sounding off over nothing.

"I'll hunt up Kerim. You're nicer to me when he's around."

"I'll help," I said to make up with her. "I haven't seen him since we left the cave." I checked out the sinks and up and down the tables. Surely he would be here in a minute. I was certain he had left the cave with the rest of us—well, almost certain. I was worried for a reason. Coming out of the cave just now, I had seen that pinpoint of light again to the right of the entrance. I tried to tell myself that it was a wisp of light from Dad's flashlight playing against the blackness, but I knew it was not.

Somehow I made it through lunch, although Kerim never showed up. This wasn't like him. He always ate lunch and usually hid food in his shirt and ran off afterward. Once he had headed toward the cave with the food, but I never said anything about it. Where was he now? Was he all right? Nobody else but me seemed concerned about him.

"Where's Kerim?" Jennifer asked after our meal.

"I don't know, nosy. Maybe he went home." Couldn't she see I was already worried sick about him?

"I don't like you, Jeff, when you call me nosy."

"I don't like you either when you ask stupid questions."

"So what's stupid about it?"

"I don't know."

128

*Coming out of the cave, I saw
a pinpoint of light.*

"Well, if you don't know—"

"Will you please stop?" I yelled.

I looked up to see Mom staring at us.

"Jeff, come with me to our tent. Jennifer, go take your shower."

I was in for it now. I scuffed at the rocks along the path. If I hadn't gotten into trouble with Mom, I could go look for Kerim. I knew I could not take the four-hour afternoon rest without knowing he was all right.

Inside the tent I had my mind so much on Kerim I didn't pay attention to Mom's verbal spanking until she said, "I know something is bothering you, Jeff. Every time you get up-tight about one thing or another, you start treating Jennifer like the dirt under your feet."

I opened my mouth to protest, but she continued: "It may be too much to ask a 12-year-old to grow up, Jeff. But at some time you'll have to learn how to settle the thing that is *really* bothering you without taking it out on Jennifer." She turned and headed for the showers.

I sat on my cot, feeling miserable. All right, I thought, I'll settle what's really bothering me! But right then my worry was Kerim, so I decided I would have to postpone my misery until I had found him. I looked out to be sure Jennifer and Dad were not coming down the path; then I grabbed a towel so they would think I was on my way to the showers if I ran into them. I rolled

Dad's flashlight and the slingstone Mom had given me into the towel and dashed out of the tent.

"Watch it, kid!" Hank exclaimed as I rounded the corner.

"I will! I will!" He'd better not delay me.

At the showers I turned and headed out the gate to the fields, praying that no one would see me and call me back. This was the first time I had struck out alone. I wouldn't really go into the cave by myself, I kept thinking over and over. The important thing was to get there. I looked out toward the Bedouin camp but Kerim was nowhere in sight.

Running down the hillside, I slipped and fell, but I finally reached the cave. I peered into its big black mouth and saw nothing.

I could hear Dad's firm voice, as strong as if he were saying it right in my ear: "Do not go into the cave alone." Kerim could be home resting or tending the animals. Or he might be somewhere on the tell by now. I was stupid. What was I doing here anyway? Turning my back on the cave and gazing out on the plain, I shifted the flashlight and slingstone in the towel to my left hand, then reached down and picked up a rock to throw.

I stared. Drawn on the rocky soil beside the entrance to the cave was the distinct outline of a fish. Danger! I wanted to run for my life, but my feet were glued to the ground. My head pounded.

131

Kerim had said danger is near if you ever see the sign of a fish. I stared at it . . . The head of the fish was facing the cave. Did that mean anything?

The sun beat down on me, hotter than ever before. I wiped the sweat gushing down my face and neck with an end of the towel, then I unwrapped the flashlight.

"O God," I prayed, "I don't want to disobey Dad. I want him and Mom to believe in me and trust me, but if I do the wrong thing, Mom and Dad—" I shut my eyes against what they would think. "But Kerim needs me. I know he does. I made him a promise about the fish, and now I don't know what to do. Do You know what to do, God?"

I hoped God could understand prayers that didn't make much sense.

Flashing through my memory came Kerim's words: If I saw the sign of the fish, I must get help and *then* find him. I glanced up toward the deep blue sky and hoped that was my answer.

I blinked. At the top of the tell, with her chin propped on her knees, sat Jennifer staring down at me.

Inside the Cave

15

Inside the Cave

I DROPPED MY BELONGINGS on top of the fish design and dashed up the hillside.

"Am I glad to see you! Now, Jen, listen carefully—"

"Jeff, you're white like my Easter bunny. You're going to have a sunstroke."

"No, Jen, just listen."

I dug my pottery sherd out of my pocket and laid it in her palm. "Jen, I'm giving this back to you so you'll know it is important for you to do exactly what I say."

"OK, Jeff." Her big brown eyes widened in fright. She must have felt how scared I was.

My words couldn't tumble out fast enough. "I am going into the cave—no, no, don't say anything. I think Kerim is in some kind of danger. I'm going in alone because if I wait for someone to come it may be too late. But you're to run and tell Dad I've gone inside and that he is to get help and come down fast. Tell him to be careful—and tell him, Jen, he's to turn to the *right* inside the cave, not left. Have you got that?"

She nodded, one big tear rolling down her cheek. I rubbed it away with my thumb.

"Hurry now, we have to think about Kerim."

She pressed the sherd back into my hand. "You keep it for love energy, Jeff. I'll do everything you said."

She raced toward the other side of the tell. I moved cautiously back down the hill, mopping my face on my shirt. The slingstone was still wrapped in the towel. I checked the flashlight to be sure it was working, then I moved inside the cave. When its cool shade struck me I shivered.

I kept the flashlight off and moved snail-like. Where the cave curved to the left toward our diggings, I turned to the right and gazed into midnight blackness as if my eyes had been punched out. I waited and listened, afraid to turn on my light. At first all I could hear was my heart thudding against my ribs. Then a scurrying sound—like field mice on the run—came through the dark. I had to get my mind off my own danger—if there were any—and think only about Kerim.

Finally, with the light turned toward the ground, I moved the switch—my thumb stiff against it. I forced my arm up slowly so that the light split the darkness straight ahead. A plain cave wall ten feet ahead stared back at me. I crept down the passageway. Where the cave curved to the left, I drew a fish on the wall with my sherd to give me direction for going back. Then I inched along the passage.

The passage was endless. Finally a stone wall stopped me. I raised the light and discovered that the wall was cut away about three feet from the ceiling and exposed another passage at the higher level. I climbed the rock wall, clinging to the jutting stones and using them for steps, then I drew another fish on the ceiling and crawled on my hands and knees down the narrow upper passage.

Several new smells hit me—not the moldy odor of the passage—but the smell of sheep, of gunpowder, of smoke . . . I wanted to turn back but instead I shut off the light and shuffled ahead, my fingers sliding along the floor to guide me. By now I had hitched the slingstone inside the back of my pants, lost the towel from around my neck, and clamped my teeth around the handle of the flashlight. The ragged edges of the sherd cut into my hand. I must remember the way I had come. I drew another fish on the floor although I could not see it. A pale light seeped through the passage ahead. The smell of smoke was stronger.

Suddenly I came out into a large cave chamber and stood up. Stones encircled a small fire. Pottery jugs stood nearby. The only light was from the fire, flickering against the walls.

My gaze shifted cautiously around the room.

"Kerim!" I said. All caution left me. I dashed across to the opposite side beyond the fire where he lay in a heap. He did not move.

"Kerim! Kerim!" I put my head on his chest to listen for his heartbeat. I was sure he was dead.

I froze when he whispered: "My arms are tied behind me. Keep your head on my chest."

I stayed there motionless. He whispered again, "I was knocked unconscious. *He* thinks I still am."

Who? I wondered. I had seen no one else, but I was afraid to ask. I moved to pick Kerim up when a voice echoed through the chamber. I whirled around although I could not understand the foreign words.

Facing me was a young man—not much older than Kerim—with a rifle in his hand. A Palestinian guerrilla!

"I have to get my friend out! Don't you understand that? I must get him out!" I shouted, moving back toward Kerim.

The stranger snarled, and motioned with his gun for me to stay where I was. How could I call his bluff?

I gestured wildly. "My friend is dying! I must get him out!"

An evil grin crossed his dark face. I lunged for the fire to beat it out with a stone. Perhaps Kerim and I could get away in the darkness. The guerrilla aimed his rifle at my chest, then suddenly swung the butt at my head. I lurched backward just in time to miss the blow. Snarling again, he motioned me away from the fire with the butt of the rifle. I crawled back to Kerim and laid my head on his chest, feeling his pulse at his wrist.

"We'll find a way," I whispered. "Help is coming."

"Be careful!"

Another snarl. I had to move away from Kerim; the guerrilla was telling me with a motion of the rifle. I did. Shaking my head to clear it, I realized he wasn't going to fire that gun! Of course not. He was afraid that it would be heard outside the cave. If I could stamp the fire out he would have no light. I wanted to lunge for it again, but the sick grin on his face stopped me. I had read that guerrillas did not put a high price on their own lives. This one might be willing to risk shooting the gun if I pressed him—a shot for each of us.

"Sometimes you're too impulsive for your own good," Mom had told me once.

I sat and waited.

Finally I could not stand the silence, the eerie flickers on the walls, the gun pointed at my forehead. Dad must be coming with help; could he hear me if I shouted?

I began to talk loudly—gibberish, anything that came into my mind—as I kept my gaze fastened on the gunman. Kerim did not move.

139

"I hear a noise!" I yelled. "It's mice! It's rats! No, it's little black kittens!" I yelled till I was exhausted.

The guerrilla knew. He *had* to know that way back in this dark room no one could hear me if I shouted till doomsday. When I turned my head from side to side, the rifle moved back and forth with my movements. His hateful grin told me he was enjoying my torture.

I cautiously moved my hands behind me to reach the slingstone lodged under my belt. Clamping my fingers around the stone, I pointed toward the entrance with my free hand and screamed, "Watch out! Watch out! He has a gun!"

The guerrilla jerked and opened fire on the entrance. I flashed my light into his eyes to blind him and heaved the slingstone at his head.

He fell.

I dashed to Kerim.

"Knife in my pocket—" he gasped. "Cut the ropes!"

I reached for the knife. A loud splintering sound above us shattered the silence. We crouched together looking upward. Light streamed in from an opening in the roof of the cave chamber.

"Jeff! Kerim! Jeff!" Jennifer's shout was the sweetest sound I had ever heard.

Linked by the Fish

16

Linked by the Fish

I DON'T KNOW WHY YOU FAINTED after you were safe," Jennifer said, sitting on the edge of my cot in the nurse's tent.

"I was scared, Jen."

"And you wouldn't be hurt at all if you hadn't held that piece of pottery so tight."

I looked at my bandaged hand. "I needed lots of your love energy," I said. I figured as long as my sister was sentimental, I could be too. "Is Kerim okay?"

"He's right over there."

I was so relieved I could have cried at the sight of Kerim across the tent on another cot. He looked just as happy as I felt but he didn't say anything. I knew he wasn't going to say any sticky words about my coming in the cave to find him. He knew they would just make me feel funny.

"Boy, I'm glad to see you," I said.

"I knew you would come, Jeff, when you missed me at lunch."

He *knew* I would come.

Mom and Dad were standing in the doorway. They didn't say anything, but I didn't feel any shame about going into the cave alone. It seemed right. For once I trusted my own decision. I hoped they would understand but if they didn't, I knew it was exactly as Mom had said the night I left Jennifer alone last year. They might be disappointed in me for what I had done, but they still loved me. I didn't know it then, but I certainly did now.

They came inside and sat on stools beside me.

"I had to go in the cave alone, Dad, but not before I sent for you."

"And you were right," Dad said. "As soon as Jennifer told me you had gone in, I knew you had decided it was the thing you had to do."

He *knew*. He had trusted me.

"A tough decision for a 12-year-old," Dad added.

"Jennifer made it easier by following me to the cave. If she hadn't, I would have had to go up on the tell for help." I hesitated before I added, "It was because of the fish that I hunted for Kerim."

Dad looked completely surprised. "What's this fish business?"

"Do you remember what you said at Capernaum about us being linked to Jesus and other people of long ago by faith?"

He nodded.

"Well, Kerim and I were linked by the sign of a fish."

"I'm just thankful you and Kerim are safe now," Mom said.

"It could have been different," added Kerim from his cot.

Dad's voice was low. "Yes. Sometimes we don't know if a decision is good or bad when we must make it. We just have to trust, don't we, Jeff?"

They understood. I looked from Dad to Mom. "Thanks," I mumbled, my throat suddenly scratchy.

"All the shouting you did, Jeff, pinpointed where you were," Mom explained. "We could hear you above ground, and Mr. Mac knew exactly how to get there from above to save time."

"From above?"

"Through a tunnel dug years ago by archaeologists. We passed through a stone shaft that led into a cistern—"

"Which had an opening to that cave room," Jennifer interrupted.

"I am glad Mr. Mac knew about that entrance," added Kerim. So was I. It was a simple one compared to the long torturous route along the passages we had come through.

Now that I knew how my parents felt about

what I had done, I was eager to know what had happened after I passed out.

"I didn't kill the guerrilla, did I?"

"No."

I shuddered at the memory of his evil face but was glad that I didn't kill him. He had been tied up with Kerim's ropes, Mom said, and was now in the custody of the military. Soldiers were already spread out in the mountains around the tell, hunting the rest of the band.

"But we aren't in danger now or they would evacuate the tell," she reassured us.

"What were the guerrillas doing here?"

"Hiding out—no one would suspect them of being on a tell where there were so many people. At night they moved out undetected to raid the countryside. They just happened to find a perfect hideout in an unexcavated section of the cave."

"How did you get into this, Kerim?" I was as full of questions as Jennifer.

He said, "One day I followed the pinpoint of light I saw at that end of the cave."

"That's what I saw! What was it?"

Mr. Mac entered the tent in time to answer. "This cave system is intricate and interlaced with cisterns and tunnels built to bring in water underground from a source outside the city walls. It is impossible to know where that tiny spot of light came from in all that labyrinth."

He sounded like a teacher. I grinned at Dad.

"I wish I had not seen that light!" Kerim said. It led him accidentally onto the guerrilla band. They then blackmailed him into bringing them food and keeping their hideout a secret.

"If I had not," Kerim added and his eyes filled with new fear, "they showed me the grenades they would use. They would blow up the tell, they said, and my people's tent homes, even if they killed themselves when they did it."

"Kerim—"

"I was afraid, Jeff, that they could hear everything I said even when they were far away. That is why I did not speak with you freely about the cave."

"All those strange conversations!"

"I could not let you talk about the cave. They might overhear and think that I gave them away."

"Who was the man in Tiberias?"

"One of this band. Two of them had gone there to connect up with another band. When he accidentally bumped into me, he was suspicious about why I was there. He threatened me. And then you saw him—and he saw you—and I was frightened for everyone here."

I was thoroughly confused. "But—but I don't understand how you got yourself tied up down in the cave."

Kerim was suddenly tongue-tied. Finally he said, "I love my land. I love my people."

"I still don't understand."

He was groping for words. "I—I stayed behind today at lunch. I went to the hideout to tell them that I will not bring them food again. That they must leave. That I cannot help men who kill the people of my land—"

"But you are an Arab too!" I said.

"Not a guerrilla! I made my decision," he said firmly. "My life I can lose—that is nothing. But I do not live another day in fear and shame that I am slave to evil men who kill my people."

No wonder he seldom smiled.

I said, "There's the sign of a fish along those cave walls for direction. They'll be there forever."

"I love my land," Kerim said again, his eyes lighting up with excitement. "The Jews love my land. Christians and Muslims love my land. It must be the best place on earth."

I smelled the dust on this desert tell and said, "It must be."

Kerim raised himself up from his cot. "But I will not kill. I wish my whole land were like the people who work together right here."

Jennifer and I exchanged glances. We had once said the same thing.

"To think that the guerrillas making raids at Tel Aviv yesterday were living right under us," Mom said.

I shuddered.

"They could have turned us into goofers!" Jennifer grinned at me and slung her *ibrik* up for a drink.

They held us in the nurse's tent overnight for observation although Kerim and I were aching to go home. His mother and father came in the evening when his father returned from work in the valley. I could not understand what they said but I did not need to.

Mom never left the side of my cot. Sometimes as I dozed off to sleep I could feel her rubbing my back as she did when I was little and couldn't go to sleep. Sometimes she rubbed Kerim's back too.

The next day we stayed so busy I hardly saw Jennifer. Soldiers were in and out of the unexcavated tunnels, clearing out ammunition left by the guerrillas, asking Kerim and me and Mr. Mac and others a million questions. I did not know much to report, but I learned a lot by listening to everyone else.

It was late afternoon when I hunted out Jennifer.

"Let's go sit on the other side of the tell," I said.

We didn't say anything all the way over. We sat on the edge, threw pebbles down the slope, and gazed out across the plains.

I wanted to talk to her but couldn't find a way to say what I felt, so I took the pottery sherd she had given me out of my pocket and drew a fish on the ground beside us.

"What's that for?"

"Oh, I like to think Jesus once walked here just like King Solomon and David did hundreds of years before Him."

Jennifer took the pottery sherd and studied the stick figures. Mr. Nebergall had said that someday I would be able to "read that gift for myself." In a sense I figured I already could because of the giver.

"I sure am glad nosy old Jennifer followed me to the cave yesterday," I said.

"Huh! I knew you weren't supposed to be out there during rest time."

"I can depend on you to tag along after me."

She looked hurt.

"It's a compliment," I said quickly. "I needed you and you were there."

"Oh!" She brightened and handed my sherd back to me.

I had not said what I wanted to very well, but we gazed out from our tell. Suddenly we didn't need to talk. The view over the Mediterranean Sea was magnificent with its fiery red sunset.

The artillery-shell gong sounded for the evening lecture. Kerim lifted the shovel to bong it again.

I turned and challenged Jennifer.

"Race you across the tell!" I said.

The Wonderful World of Children's Books

❝ Reading about a character is a lot different than seeing him on TV. You can get to know him better—get more deeply involved with him as a person—in a book, because you're with him a lot longer. **❞**

Barbara Reeves, consultant to "Sesame Street"

IN GRANDMA'S ATTIC. Ever explore an attic? It's lots of fun—especially when the strange items one finds cause grandma to tell neat stories about the olden days. Fifty years ago, in a big farm house in Michigan, a girl used to explore her grandma's attic . . . and ask questions about the strange things she found. The stories her grandma told are in this book: how a beaded basket led to a scary adventure with a hungry Indian . . . the time grandma took a dare, and nearly froze her tongue on the new pump . . . why grandpa was so positive the shoes a neighbor offered him would fit, because "when the Lord sends me shoes, he sends the right size." 77271—$1.25

Handy order form on last page

The Wonderful World of Pop-Up Books

Favorite Bible stories that "Pop Up" . . . full-color scenes, often three dimensional . . . figures lift from the scene when page is turned . . . other figures move when tabs are pulled.

The Shepherds' Surprise. Child opens book, and shepherds raise up from the page . . . child pulls tab, and angel appears in the clouds.   82362—$3.95

The Life of Moses. Hebrew slaves push a big stone, chariot moves, bush burns, waters part . . . all as child turns pages, pulls tabs, etc.   82370—$3.95

Jesus Lives! Gethsemane scene appears in 3D as book opens . . . Jesus appears in upper room when tab is pulled . . . He ascends into clouds as page turns.
    82388—$3.95

Noah's Animal Boat. Amazing action—Noah's saw moves and sounds . . . animals and ark appear in 3-D . . . ark tosses on the waves. More, too!   82396—$3.95

Handy order form
on last page

The Wonderful World of Teen Paperbacks

Fire! You'll find mystery in this tale of Ann and Rob, who spend a summer with their aunt and forest-ranger uncle. They look forward to adventure, but they find more than they really want. Can the two teenagers help discover who is starting the forest fires? More important, can they help lead their unbelieving uncle to a greater discovery?   82974—$1.25

Tanya and the Border Guard. Tanya lives in Russia, where visible Christians are often persecuted. When her family and friends worship, they must gather secretly in a forest. Was Tanya wise to reveal their meeting place to the soldier, even though he did say he was a believer? She'll soon find out—because now he and two more soldiers appear at their little meeting in the forest!   75994—$1.25

Alexi's Secret Mission. For Christian activities, Alexi's family is banished to Siberia. Alexi has to give up his friends; worse yet, he can't be on the school team because he's a Christian. He almost resents his faith! But soon he's involved in something more exciting than sports—spreading God's Word. And what does that service to God bring him? Read fast!   87338—$1.25

Turkey Red. When Martha's farming family came to America for religious freedom, they brought a special variety of wheat—red wheat. It grew well in Kansas, but no one would buy red wheat. Brother Jake had other troubles: prairie fires, rattlesnakes, Indians; so he ran away to the city. And for Martha . . . a real problem of the time: should she mix with children who didn't belong to their church? Important lessons in sharing!   89482—$1.25

Handy order form on last page

The Wonderful World of Teen Paperbacks

Never Miss A Sunset. Put yourself in Ellen's place: 75 years ago, on a backwoods farm in Wisconsin. Ellen is 13. She loves her family, but resents being second mother to her nine brothers and sisters. Then tragedy brings Ellen a guilt heavier than all her chores —a terrible burden that remains until winter warms into spring . . . to bring a time of new understanding for Ellen and her mother.   86512—$1.95

City Kid Farmer. Won first prize in David C. Cook's 1975 children's book contest! You'll sympathize with Mark; he has to give up his friends when his folks move to the country. But worse, his aunt and uncle are just as "religious" as his mother. You'll see how Mark adjusts to rural life . . . and the chain of events that leads him to know Christ himself.   89474—$1.25

Pounding Hooves. More than an exciting horse story— it's the story of Lori's jealous struggle with her friend Darlene. Darlene probably will win the art contest. She'll win Ken, too—Darlene's so pretty! And Storm, the beautiful Arabian stallion—Darlene's father surely will buy him before Lori saves enough money. Rivals for so much . . . even with God's help, can Lori overcome her jealousy of Darlene?   89458—$1.75

Captured! Teenage adventure in wilderness America! Captured by Indians, Crist and Zack strike a bargain. The Indians want to learn more about the white man's ways, so the boys agree to teach the Indians—if they will spare their lives. But the boys would rather return home. Why, then, does Crist pass up a chance to escape? And Zack—why does he escape . . . then act so strangely when he finds the chief's son wounded, and helpless?   87312—$1.50

Handy order form on last page

The Wonderful World of Picture Strip Books

The Adventures of Tullus, teenage Christian in ancient Rome. Tullus fights for his faith against the terrors of his time. Exciting adventures in black-and-white picture strips, with fast-moving dialogue! Each book 112 pages.

Tullus and the Ransom Gold. Can Tullus find enough money to free his Christian friends from death in the arena? He does —but then finds himself in the arena . . . defending a girl from a savage lion. What can he do!   77057—$1.25

Tullus and the Vandals of the North. Go with Tullus as he explores the outer limits of the ancient Roman empire . . . see how faith and prayer help him turn trials into opportunities to win others for Christ.   81249—$1.25

Tullus and the Kidnapped Prince. Would you risk your life for a savage young prince in faraway India? Tullus does. See why!   84152—$1.25

Tullus in the Deadly Whirlpool. Can Tullus convince the sailors he's not to blame for the storm and whirlpool that threaten their ship? He must convince them. But how?   77065—$1.25

Boxed gift set of 4 books. $4.95

Christian Family Classics. Two famous stories—"Ben Hur," and "Christian Family Courageous." Learn how a youth in Bible times overcame tremendous adversity. Read how a shipwrecked family provided for its needs on a tropic island. Both stories told in black-and-white picture strips, dialogue, captions.   81786—$1.25

Handy order form on last page

The Wonderful World of The Picture Bible

Easiest way imaginable to read the Bible—all the drama and excitement unfold vividly in black-and-white picture strips, easy-to-read dialogue, and captions.

All illustrations and statements authenticated by Bible scholars for biblical and cultured accuracy. Enjoy reading these 6 volumes:

OLD TESTAMENT

Creation: From "In the beginning" to the flight from Egypt

The Promised Land: Moses, Ten Commandments, Jericho

The Captivity: Divided kingdom falls . . . Israel is taken into captivity . . . prophecies of a coming Messiah

NEW TESTAMENT

Jesus: The Life of our Lord—His birth, ministry, first followers, crucifixion, and triumph over death

The Church: Angels announce Jesus will return . . . Pentecost . . . Stephen is stoned . . . Paul's conversion, missionary ministry, and death . . . the end of an era.

82701—All 6 books in slipcase. Set, $6.95

Handy order form on last page

The Wonderful World of Magic Picture Books

Bible stories—plus! Each book tells a favorite Bible story in words children 4-8 understand and love. Every page has a full-color illustration, and also a "magic" blank spot that's a source of surprise and delight when rubbed with a pencil.

BIBLE STORIES

Set 1: One! Two! and You ● Here's My Donkey ● Strange New Star ● Jonah ● God Made It Good ● Ruth's New Home   70920—$1.95

Set 2: What Shepherds Saw ● Up the Sycamore Tree ● Ring, Robe and Shoes ● Colorful Coat ● David, the Giant Killer ● In a Lions' Den   70938—$1.95

Set 3: Down Through the Roof ● Lost Lamb ● Night Ride to Egypt ● Jericho ● Gideon's Warriors ● Baby Moses   70946—$1.95

Set 4: The Birth of Jesus ● Jesus Lives! ● Noah's Ark ● Queen Esther ● Why Seas Grew Calm ● Shadrach, Meshach, and Abednego   70953—$1.95

LIFE RELATED STORIES

Set 101: Ranger Treemore's Flowers ● Rabbit That Changed Colors ● Frisky's Christmas Tree ● Ants! ● Bear of a Different Color ● A Special Treat.   86934—$1.95

Set 102: Too Many Blackberries ● Lolly and the Christmas Cactus ● Frisky Pup Playing Possum ● Katy's Kittens ● No Eggs for Barney ● Why the Fish Grew   86942—$1.95

When a child rubs a pencil over one of the blank spots, a story-related activity appears. It may be a drawing, words, dot-to-dot puzzle, crossword puzzle, etc.

Handy order form on last page

The Wonderful World of Children's Books

THE SHAWL OF WAITING

Maybe you'd have done the same, if your grandmother had told you such a strange story. Anyway, after hearing her grandma's story, Emilie Coulter started to knit her own "shawl of waiting." Emilie knit, and knit—even if she didn't believe her grandma's story. But the more Emilie knit, the smaller the shawl became! Why couldn't she finish it? 89466—$1.25